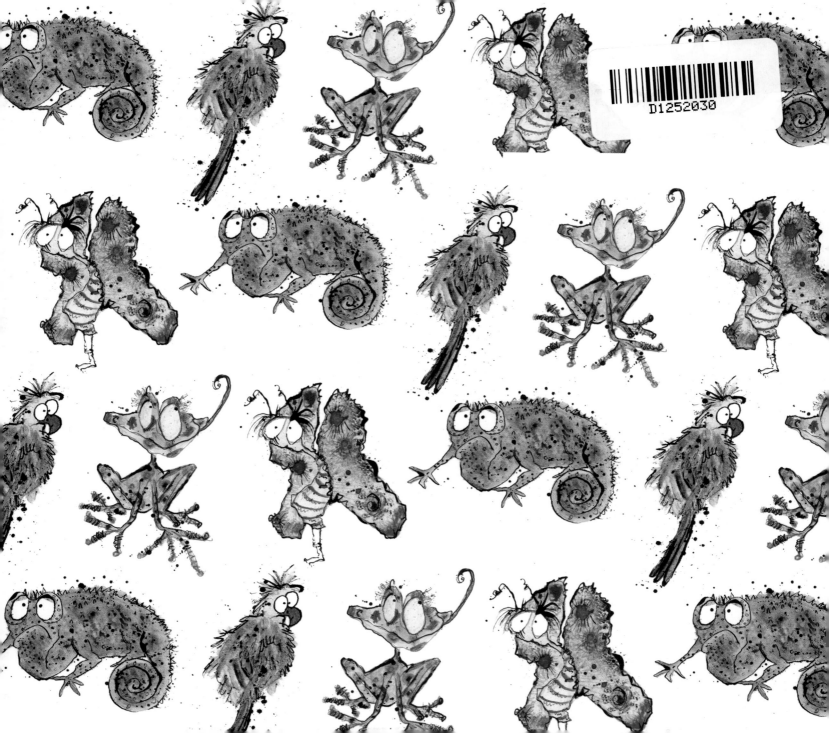

ZOE AND HER ZANY ANIMALS

Published in Great Britain and the United States in 2006 by
MARION BOYARS PUBLISHERS LTD
24 Lacy Road, London SW15 1NL
www.marionboyars.co.uk

Distributed in Australia and New Zealand by Peribo Pty Ltd
58 Beaumont Road, Kuring-gai, NSW 2080

Printed in 2006
10 9 8 7 6 5 4 3 2 1

A CIP catalogue record for this book is available from the British Library.
A CIP catalog record for this book is available from the Library of Congress.

ISBN 0-7145-3306-8
13 digit ISBN 978-0-7145-3306-3

Set in Bell 20/26 pt
Printed in China

ZOE AND HER ZANY ANIMALS

Illustrated by Marjorie Dumortier

MARION BOYARS
CHILDREN'S

Welcome friends! My name is Zoe and I'm on my first trip to the jungle.

Come and see the zany animals with me. I am here to tell you about some of my favourites.

Lions, tigers, monkeys and crocodiles, all of these animals prowl the jungle – watch out! But I want to show you some even more exotic creatures. Are you ready?

I guess you know there is such a thing as a zebra, covered in black and white stripes from head to toe. And lots of you have enjoyed rides on donkeys…

...but have you ever heard of a **ZEDONK**?

Lions are my favourite animals as they
are the lords of the animal kingdom.
I like tigers because of their stripes too.

But have you ever seen a **LIGER**?

Sometimes I see cows when I am on the plains and huge buffalo swimming in the river.

But one day, if I wish hard enough, perhaps I'll see some **BEEFALO**!
You never know.

There are sheep in the camp, whose wool is used to make warm blankets. And as goatskin can make good strong bags to carry water, there are goats too.

Imagine what you could get from a cross breed – a **GEEP**!

Another useful creature would be a mix of a dog and a desert coyote. At night he could guard the campsite, in a growling, snappy coyote way, and in the day he could be a lovable pet.

Anyone else think they might like a **DOGOTE**?

There are other zany
animals here too, but the
lynx and scraggy
wild cat are the most
fun to play with.

Imagine how much fun a **CATYNX** would be.
Can you spot which half is which?

With its long legs and humps full of water, Zoe loves to ride high up on the camel. But do you know what a mixture of the camel and the llama looks like?

Guess what, we found a beautiful CAMA.

When Zoe's had enough of the hot, dry desert and the steamy jungle, she dives straight into the sea. Are there any zany sea creatures in the ocean? She can see a cross between a killer whale and a bottle-nose dolphin. It can only be…

...a WOLPHIN.

Ha! My grandmother told me she once saw a mix between a liontail monkey and a pigtail monkey. Do you think she was making it up?

She can't decide which nutty name is better for the mix
of these two creatures. Which name do you prefer – a
CONKEY or a **LONKEY**?

A ZORSE?

Zoe thinks there may be other mixed up animals. Can you think of some that she doesn't know?

A PUMPAPARD?

Let's think of some more...   like the **FLAMINGUIN**,

the
HIPPOGATOR

and the **SNAKIZARD**.

Scariest of all, one day Zoe may come across a mix of a person and a chimpanzee…

the **HUMANZEE!**

Time for Zoe to leave the jungle and the plains and the ocean. She'll have to be careful on her way home, you never know what she may bump into...

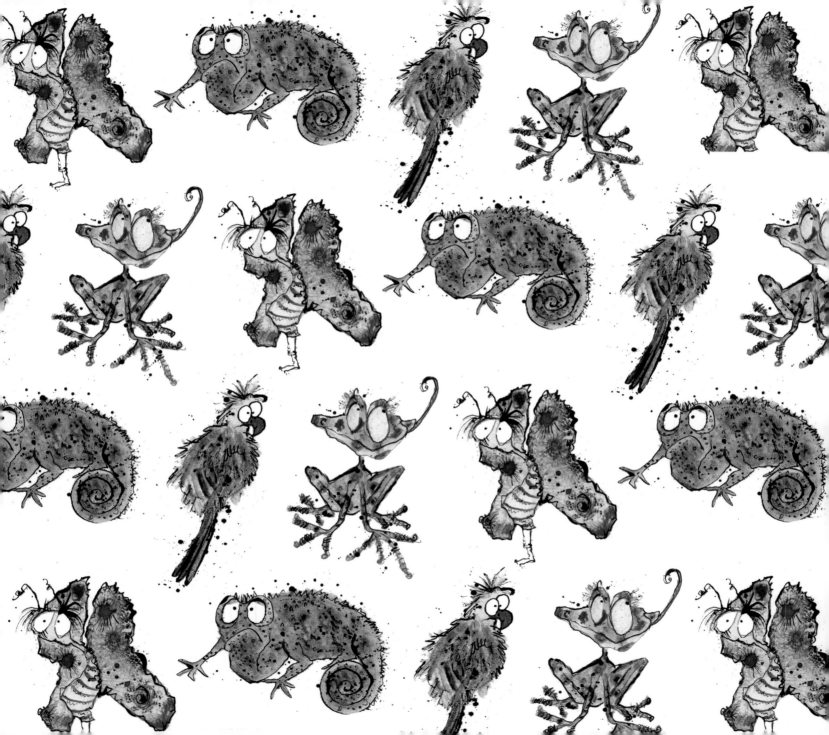